It's Okay to Be Different

Todd Parr

Megan Tingley Books
LITTLE, BROWN AND COMPANY
New York — Boston

To Megan
for believing in something different
Love,
Todd

Little, Brown Books for Young Readers

Hachette Book Group
237 Park Avenue, New York, NY 10017
Visit our Web site at www.lb-kids.com

Little, Brown Books for Young Readers is a division of Hachette Book Group, Inc.
The Little, Brown name and logo are trademarks of Hachette Book Group, Inc.

First Paper Over Board Edition: May 2004

Library of Congress Cataloging-in-Publication Data

Parr, Todd.
  It's okay to be different / by Todd Parr. — 1st ed.
    p. cm
    Summary: Illustrations and brief text describe all kinds of differences that are
"okay," such as "It's okay to be a different color," "It's okay to need some help,"
"It's okay to be adopted," and "It's okay to have a different nose."
    ISBN 978-0-316-15562-5
    [1. Self-esteem — Fiction. 2. Individuality — Fiction.] I. Title
PZ7.P2447 It 2001
[E] — dc21   00-042829

10 9 8 7 6 5

TWP

Printed in Singapore

It's okay to be
missing a tooth
(or two or three)

It's okay to have a
different nose

It's okay to be a different color

It's okay to have BIG ears

It's okay to have wheels

It's okay to be

Small

Medium

Large   Extra Large

It's okay to
wear glasses

It's okay to eat
macaroni and cheese
in the bathtub

It's okay to say NO
to bad things

I's okay to be embarrassed

It's okay to have a pet worm

It's okay to have different
Moms

It's okay to have different
Dads

It's okay to be adopted

It's okay to have an invisible friend

It's okay to do something nice for someone

It's okay to lose
your mittens

It's okay to get mad

It's okay to help a
squirrel collect nuts

It's okay to have different kinds of friends

It's okay to make a wish

It's Okay to be different. You are special and Important just because of being who you are.

Love,
Todd